For Dana

Library of Congress Cataloging-in-Publication Data.
Stock, Catherine.   Birthday present   /   by Catherine
Stock.   —   1st ed.   p.   cm.   Summary:
Although he is not pleased with his mother's choice of gift
for him to take to a birthday party, a little boy attends and
experiences a pleasant surprise.   ISBN 0-02-788401-5
[1. Birthdays—Fiction.   2. Parties—Fiction.]   I. Title.
PZ7.S8635Bi   1991   [E]—dc20   90-1914   CIP   AC

Birthday Present

BY CATHERINE STOCK

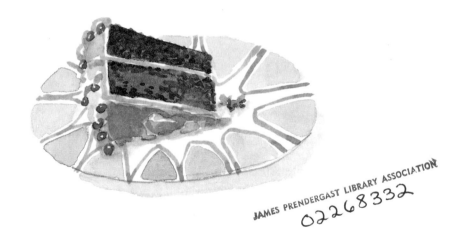

BRADBURY PRESS · NEW YORK

COLLIER MACMILLAN CANADA
Toronto
MAXWELL MACMILLAN INTERNATIONAL PUBLISHING GROUP
New York   Oxford   Singapore   Sydney

A letter arrives for me.
It's an invitation to a birthday party from my friend Maria.

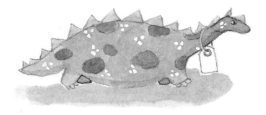

Mommy and I go to find a present
for Maria.

I want to buy her a green spider
that glows in the dark, a car that
turns into a space monster, and a
gorilla mask.

But Mommy buys her a blue ball
with yellow spots.

On the day of the party I get ready.
I wear a plaid jacket and a green
bow tie.

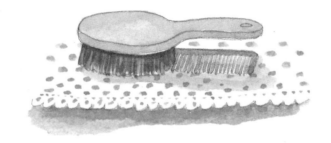

We go to Maria's house.
Simon, Georgie, and Alice are already there.

In the middle of the table is a pink cake with four candles.

Maria makes a wish and blows out the candles.

Then we eat ice cream, cake, and Jell-O.

It's time to open the presents.
Simon's present is a green
spider that glows in the dark.

Georgie's present is a car that
turns into a space monster.

Alice's present is a gorilla mask.

Maria opens my present.
  "A ball! Just what I wished
for," she says.

And we all run out to the yard
to play together.